THE NAVY GIRL BOOK

Also by Scott Erickson

SATIRE

The History of the Decline and Fall of America:
A Semi-Fictional Satire.

Invasion of the Dumb Snatchers

The Diary of Amy, the 14-Year-Old
Girl Who Saved the Earth

HUMOR

Icons Are People, Too

Seventeen and Turning into a Non-Mormon
Secular Humanist Zombie

B-Movie Mash-Up: Gastropods of Terror and
How to Get a Head in Real Estate

The Best of Reality Ranch

THE
NAVY GIRL
BOOK

By Scott Erickson

If the only tool we have is a bottle of whiskey, then every problem looks like we can get drunk and forget about it.

When I was young, I dreamed of being a cowboy. Now that I have achieved my dream, I dream of starting over with a dream of being something that pays better and doesn't involve cows.

Sustaining a marriage requires falling in love over and over again, mostly with the same person.

Help create and sustain a healthy and positive work environment by making a commitment to not support workplace gossip, unlike that bitch Martha in accounting.

Do you have a girlfriend who believes the commercial that says, "Show her you love her with diamonds"? If so, dump her and find a girlfriend who equates love with something less expensive, like a sandwich.

Tomorrow is Bring Your Child to Work day! Help your children understand why every night Mommy and Daddy need to get drunk.

What are human beings? We are children of the universe, born of a planet made from the ashes of collapsed stars. We are the universe conscious of itself; we are the universe thinking about itself and whether the cute barista is single.

I was hunting elk in Wyoming when my gun jammed and the dominant male started charging me. Suddenly the hunter had become the hunted! Then an immense buffalo appeared and started charging both me and the elk. In the presence of a new hunter, suddenly we both had become the hunted! Eventually it was every living thing on earth versus Godzilla.

Hear ye! Hear ye! I am your
faithful town crier here to
announce that I must be in
a goddamn time warp.

When travelling the beautiful Oregon
Coast, be sure to visit **Reedsport**.
This lovely community calls itself
"The Gateway to the Oregon Coast."
Of course, anyplace could call itself
that. If you're coming from New
York, Nebraska could call itself the
gateway to the Oregon Coast.

In America, any child can
grow up. That's called
the American dream.

BUSINESSES THAT FAILED FOR SOME REASON

Doctor Feelgood's Gravy Emporium

Intimate Impregnations

Affordable Rodent Control and Discount Meats

Ten-Second Tan

Mr. Right Now Instant Dating Service

U-Churn Self-Serve Butter

Nip & Tuck Discount Facelifts

Studs 'n' Suds Baths For Guys

Nipple Twisters Custom Arousals

Beanpoles: Fashion for Tall & Skinny Folks

Modular Fetish Solutions

Two Amigos Thai Cuisine

Footloose and Fungus-Free Toenail Salon

Guzzler's Discount Drunkery

Hawt Dawgs Sensuous Sausages

The Short Bus Academy

Just the Tip Discount Circumcisions

Discount Profreeding

Taste of Iowa

Yeah, I killed a guy in Reno
just to watch him die. But I
also tickled a woman in Tulsa
just to watch her giggle.

SOLDIER: "Colonel, look! Hundreds of hawks, coming right at our feet!"

COLONEL: "Quick, soldiers! Remove your bunny slippers!"

A woman wants a confident man
who knows what he wants out
of life and knows how to make it
happen and can make her laugh
without taking off his pants.

ADVICE FOR TEEN BOYS
Have you ever wished you had more spending money?

There are things you can do that are more effective than begging your parents for a bigger allowance. You can earn extra money right in your own neighborhood by doing odd jobs like running drugs or providing sex for lonely widows. When you tell your parents that you're considering these money-making ideas, they'll give you a bigger allowance without begging.

My brother says he'll never understand women, but it all evens out because they won't date him.

Yes, the skirt is very expensive, but you should buy it. Just imagine when you arrive at the party and people look at you and say, "Wow, that skirt makes her shoes look cheap."

First Wednesday of every month at 6:00pm, THE CHRISTIAN COWBOY BALLADEERS perform at the First Episcopal Church. Admission is free. Or if you can't afford that, they'll pay you five dollars to come in.

Buddhism teaches us that the only way we can obtain the pancake is to let go of the waffle.

SHORT QUIZ
"Guess What I Am"

QUESTION: I have a shiny exoskeleton and four compound eyes. My diet consists of tiny insects and I need to live in a moist environment. What am I?

ANSWER: A liar.

He asked me if I'd like to go to dinner and a movie After I put my legs back together I told him that I have a policy to never date my gynecologist.

Does my butt make these jeans look fat?

MISSED CONNECTIONS

Silver Porsche Carrera
You: 30s, Armani suit, killer smile behind the wheel of that awesome car. Me: brunette, possessions in shopping cart, offered to clean your windshield for five dollars. I can think of lots of things to do that are more fun than dumpster diving. Meet for coffee? #806781

Jana's B'day Party
I showed you my rash, explained how my liver works. Where'd you go? That number you gave me was for Taco Bell. Meet for coffee? P.S. – I can whistle through my nose. #806781

Saturday, Safeway Parking Lot
Me: guy riding blue Fuji bicycle. You: brunette driving blue SUV who ran me over. Before losing consciousness I noticed your nice smile and your license number. I've retained a lawyer. Let's discuss compensation. Meet for coffee? #806781

Martini Bar on 10th
Saw you drinking chocolate martini, too shy to approach. I was the gentleman at the next table, blue jacket, red tie. I was extremely attracted to you, which must mean you're a lesbian. Why is every single woman I'm attracted to a lesbian? Is something wrong with me? #806781

Pizza Guy
I was lounging around in skimpy underwear when you showed up at the door. I asked, "Do you have something big and hot and delicious for me?" You answered, "Large Veggie, that'll be $35." I don't think you understand how this is supposed to work. Meet for coffee? #806781

Brad's Party

Me: Petite, red dress, a little wasted. You: Tall, green "Jameson" t-shirt, told me I was cute, got me pregnant. Would love to meet again to discuss favorite movies and wedding arrangements. Meet for coffee? We can discuss whether we should use a diaper service. #806781

Thanks for Saving Me!

I was on a horrible first date at the Sushi restaurant. You came over and saved me from the creep. Said you would take care of everything. And you did! The body was never found. If you don't get arrested, meet for coffee? #806781

Cute FedEx Guy

You are the super-cute delivery guy with bright blue eyes that makes my knees melt. You used to stop at my work every day. Then my company switched to UPS, so I started ordering stuff I don't need via FedEx just to see you. Now I'm broke and my apartment is full of useless shit. Meet for coffee, then a trip to the junkyard? #806781

I Like Your Financials

We work at the same Fortune 100 Corporation. You gave the end-of-quarter PowerPoint presentation, and when you stressed the importance of a hard response to a soft market, I thought I was going to climax right there. Let's get together. I'll give you a good return on your investment, guaranteed to make your market share rise. Or we could just have sex. Meet for coffee? #806781

When travelling the beautiful Oregon Coast, be sure to visit the lovely town of **Seaside**, Oregon's first seashore resort town, where the Chamber of Commerce invites you to spend a lot of money.

MY FAVORITE PICK-UP LINES

"Nice pick-up ya got there."

"Is yer pick-up fer sale?"

"What kinda mileage ya git on yer pick-up?"

I once dated an octopus. There we were, arm in arm in arm in arm. I told her, "I like you a lot, but I think you're spineless." I accused her of being greedy. She denied it and told me she's never been shellfish.

Welcome all of you, and thank you for coming to the first meeting of The Apathetic Society, as if any of you cared.

She's tall for her height.

Live for today because we might die tomorrow. Yes, you could try to cheat death by living in a satellite in synchronous orbit so the sun never sets and therefore tomorrow never comes, but eventually you'd run out of beer.

Freedom of speech must have limits. For example, it's against the law to yell "Salt!" in a theater full of slugs.

SON: "Hey mom! Look what I found inside the new neighbor!"

MOM: "That wasn't very nice. You put that nervous system back right away."

My qualifications? Well, I respond well to petting, and if you introduce me to your friends I won't put my wet nose in their crotch. Of course, I expect a generous benefit package, so let's talk chew toys.

TO ALL EMPLOYEES OF BETTY'S CAFE

Remember to wash your hands thoroughly after each visit to the bathroom and before resuming work

I seriously can't afford another fine from the Health Department. Since my husband died, this café is all I've got. Do right by me, and I'll do right by you. Here's some advice, free of charge: If a man wants to marry you and he thinks life insurance is a "waste of money" then take him to a short pier and ask him to take a long walk. Also, have you called your mother lately, just to tell her you love her? Same goes for your father, except he might be embarrassed to hear expressions of love. Unless he's drunk. If you inherited his drinking problem, admit you're powerless and open yourself to a higher power. Personally speaking, the only thing that keeps me from drinking gin is drinking tequila, but that might not be the best advice. If you're hiking in bear country, always hike with a friend that runs slower than you. Pink lipstick should only be worn if wearing pink, but I guess that advice applies only to women. For men, pink lipstick shouldn't be worn with anything. Hey, I just realized that sounds like if a man wears pink lipstick, he should be naked. Well, if a naked man wearing pink lipstick wants to distract me for a night or three, I might be receptive to such a thing. As long as he washes his hands thoroughly after each visit to the bathroom and before resuming work.

MY FRIEND IS A LIAR

I was saying goodbye to my blind friend, and he said, "See you later."

One step to a more positive life is to choose words carefully. Avoid words like "can't" and substitute words like "will." For example, instead of saying "I can't do it" say "I will fail."

We live in a litigation-happy society. For example, if somebody is walking alongside of the road and a big piece of plate glass flies off a truck and severs their head, their first thought is, "Who can I sue for this?" Their second thought is, "Is it possible to have sex without a head?"

I SWORE ON A BIBLE THAT THERE WOULD BE NO PUNS IN THIS BOOK BUT I'M NOT A CHRISTIAN

I've never installed electrical wiring
before, but I'm pretty sure I conduit.

The defendant is guilty of stealing
the historical museum pieces
because those artifacts of the case.

I'd like to make a model of the planet to
use for demonstrating earth's ecology.
Do you know where I can biosphere?

You'll never see insulation installed better
because this is asbestos it gets.

The wall isn't straight. Since you're a
carpenter I thought I'd askew about it.

You peed on the carpet? When
Dad finds out urine trouble.

I don't generally approve of insects
but I've decided to acceptance.

Can you show me how to buy plants
and flowers? I never botany before.

A more purposeful life begins by consciously pursing a meaningful goal. To assist you in achieving that goal, find a reminder—some sort of object that reminds you of your goal—such as a baseball bat. If anybody gets between you and your goal, apply your reminder.

DID YOU KNOW THAT THE PORN INDUSTRY MAKES 114 TIMES MORE MONEY THAT THE ENTIRE PUBLISHING INDUSTRY COMBINED?

Hi there, my name is Janet. I'm a book. Read me, baby. Read me all night long. Say the word, baby, and I'll spread my pages wide. I'll get you warmed up with a little prologue, then I'll… What did you say? You just want to read a book without all the dirty talk? Sorry, I was trying to compete with the porn industry.

A LOVE STORY

"Run away with me Lucia! We shall escape this small-minded village and embark upon a journey to a place where our love can bloom like a wild rose. It will not be an easy or pleasant journey, but do not be afraid my precious Lucia! For our love is strong and even if we must resort to sleeping in barns we shall have each other."

"Well yeah, unless I find a better boyfriend. Nothing personal, Rodrigo."

"Lucia! I do not understand!"

"You are full of youthful idealism yet have no experience with the practical realities of a long-term relationship, such as deciding who will wash the dishes."

"Lucia my love! It matters not who washes the dishes as long as it's not me."

"If you really loved me, Rodrigo, you'd be willing to share in the chores. Also, do you really expect me to sleep in a barn?"

"Lucia, I didn't realize you were so high-maintenance."

"I think I'll find a boyfriend that has a job."

"Maybe Maria will go out with me. She already lives in a barn."

Overwhelmed by the length and difficulty of your journey? Remember that the longest journey begins with a single step of those awesome red boots with the stiletto heels for the most stylish journey anyone has ever seen.

A SOLUTION TO A PROBLEM EXPERIENCED BY WOMEN

All women used to have the exact same amount of fun until that expression "blondes have more fun" came along. Unfortunately, the expression was widely believed. Which led to non-blonde women having less fun and getting angry at blonde women, and to blonde women resenting non-blonde women for being angry at them over a problem they didn't create. The solution to this problem is for all women to be bald so they'll be equally miserable.

TODAY'S TOP NEWS STORIES

In Washington D.C., a left-leaning politician discovered that their political views are based on having an extra-long right leg.

The U.S. Department of Agriculture reports that corn-fed cattle have less self-esteem than grass-fed cattle, but more than free-range chickens.

The nation's top maker of balloons claims that inflation is good for business.

Peter Piper was jailed for giving a copy of the "fig plucker" tongue-twister to Seashore Sally's friend Dyslexic Donna.

Whiskey activists attacked a pro-water rally for diluting the strength of their movement.

An extremely stupid criminal told officers there's no way he could have been at home watching television because he was downtown killing a guy.

According to a leading calendar manufacturer, our days are numbered.

A debate about the question of "nature versus nurture" led to a brawl at a recent meeting of Hitler clones.

Of all the scientists who unlocked
the secret of the genetic code,
only Nikolai Koltsov understood
the benefits of a good yodel.

When travelling the beautiful Oregon
Coast, be sure to visit the tiny
community of **Depoe Bay**. With the
annual Rowboat Show, the Salad
Festival, and the Duck Derby, Depoe Bay
really knows how to party.

Research shows that people
who spend their disposable
income on experiences are
happier than people who
have cirrhosis of the liver.

Doctors recommend that
parents on a diet should
never eat anything bigger
than their child's head.

When chefs are on sale it's a good
idea to stock up so you'll always
be prepared for a delicious meal
with very little effort.

Rutgers University published the
results of a study which proves
that radiation from cell phones
causes cancer in laboratory rats
who own tiny little cell phones.

QUOTES BY ARTISTS ABOUT ART

"Creativity takes courage. Also, money for paint. Can somebody loan me five bucks? I'm just ran out of chartreuse."
    —Henri Matisse

"The job of the artist is always to deepen the mystery. If people ask me what that means, I refuse to answer. This is how I deepen the mystery."
    —Francis Bacon

"Every good painter paints what he is. Or what he imagines himself to be. Or maybe it's what he's capable of becoming. Ask me again when I'm sober."
    —Jackson Pollock

"I found I could say things with color and shapes that I couldn't say any other way, because I don't know how to use words too good."
    —Georgia O'Keeffe

"The longer you look at an object, the more abstract it becomes and, ironically, the more real. Perhaps now you understand why I am unable to hold down a regular job."
    —Lucian Freud

"Painting is just another way of keeping a diary, except that saying "I'm sad" takes about 14 hours."
    —Pablo Picasso

"An artist is not paid for his labor but for his vision. Actually, I've never been paid for my vision. I've never been paid for anything."
　—James McNeill Whistler

"Every creator painfully experiences the chasm between his inner vision and its ultimate expression. Actually, less-sensitive creators don't experience the chasm quite so painfully."
　—Isaac Basheris Singer

"Painting is easy when you don't know how, but very difficult when you do. This is the exact opposite of playing the tuba."
　—Edgar Degas

"We see a painting as a static thing when truly it is a record of a journey that stopped when the painter ran out of paint."
　—Paul Gardner

"If I were called upon to define briefly the word Art, I should call it the reproduction of what the senses perceive in nature, seen through the veil of the soul, and represented by a bunch of pretty colors."
　—Paul Cezanne

I tried to commit original sin
but they've all been taken.

Overwhelmed by the length and
difficulty of your journey? Remember
that the longest journey begins with a
single step along with a scarecrow and
tin man. Stay on the yellow brick road,
and watch out for flying monkeys.

The main advantage of taking a
robot skydiving is that if the
parachute fails there are no lawsuits
unless the robot lands on somebody.

When travelling the beautiful Oregon Coast, be sure to visit the lovely beach community of **Newport**. Enjoy one of their many art and music festivals, then frolic in the waves and forget about the knowledge that someday you will cease to exist and all memories of you will be forgotten. Don't forget to sample Newport's world-famous clam chowder before you die!

The mystery of the headless woman found in the forest was solved by the discovery of a giant lesbian praying mantis.

The first fish hatchery established in the state of Washington has been in continuous operation for over 80 years and is estimated to have hosted over 100,000 acts of slimy fish love.

Burgers and cheese slices
actively dislike each other
and are forced to share the
same bun only because of
the iron hand of authority.

People that have been trapped in a
volcanic eruption and were forced to
swim in molten lava have been
surprised to discover that because of
the high density of lava their bodies are
extremely buoyant for a little while.

The Surgeon General has determined
that if you're a pregnant woman who
smokes you probably don't pay
attention to warning labels.

Are you considering getting into a *long-term relationship*? Be aware that will have to get used to a person hanging around all the time. This person will ask many questions with the expectation that you provide answers. They will most likely have needs that you will be expected to assist in satisfying.

Nobody can make you feel powerless without your permission. If somebody tries to make you feel powerless, make sure to tell them, "You need my permission to make me feel powerless." When they ask for permission, say "Yes" because it shows that you're a nice person.

I have the type of faith that can move mountains, for I believe in the power of plate tectonics.

The seminar by Dr. Robert Bennell PhD convinced me that I could only attain a meaningful life by becoming free of self-limiting beliefs. After months of deep inner work, I realized that the pursuit of material success was superficial, and that my purpose in life was to forego personal satisfaction and devote my life to reducing the hardships of the world's poor and suffering. After having this profound realization, I immediately contacted Dr. Bennell to ask how I could get back my self-limiting beliefs.

Experts in social psychology have determined that the best way to convince other people to see the truth of your ideas is to have a net worth of 300 million dollars.

When travelling the beautiful Oregon Coast, be sure to visit **Waldport**. This delightful seaside community is promoted as "the place where the ocean meets the sea" by a local resident who's not the sharpest tool in the shed.

The luxurious sensation of sleeping beneath satin sheets is experienced by only two percent of people who drink Coors lite.

Andrea Tanner, Realtor
andreat@remax.net

LUXURIOUS PAYETTE LAKEFRONT SETTING. Fall in love with this bright and cheery lakefront condo and the realtor that sells it to you. Just blocks from downtown McCall where I enjoy being taken on romantic dinners. Dreamy master bedroom perfect for sensuous lovemaking. 3BD, 3BA. Roomy and comfortable, condo is also very nice. $725,000 MLS#517283

BREATHTAKING VIEWS. Perfect for the man who has everything except for a loving wife and a 3BD, 2BA Greystone Village townhome. Room for two in the private hot tub. Am I being too forward? You know what you want, and so do I. You want a spiral staircase and granite tile kitchen and baths. But that's not all you want. $475,000 MLS#517283

LOCATION! LUXURY! 3BD, 3BA townhouse just a block from Payette Lake & marina. The thing is, nobody told me that being a realtor means working 70-hour weeks. I haven't had a weekend off in months. I want somebody to take care of me. What's wrong with a woman going after what she wants? Seems to be just fine when a man does it. Propane fireplace, central air-conditioning. $425,000 MLS#517283

BEST VALUE ON CASCADE LAKE. Includes basement "man cave" where you can retreat when I get too clingy. Not that I'm demanding or anything. I'm actually very low-maintenance, just like this cozy 3BD, 2BA home on a large wooded lot with landscaped yard and roomy deck. I don't like housework so we'll need a service. $214,900 MLS#517283

IT'S NOT ALWAYS EASY
BEING THE SON OF GOD

Jesus turned the water into
wine, but then local winemakers
complained this was cutting
into their profit margins.

When travelling the beautiful Oregon Coast, be
sure to visit the *Seymour Butts Memorial
Wayside*. Originally nicknamed by local
teenage boys, the name became official before
anybody figured it out. The wayside also
provides access to *I.P. Freeley State Beach*.

Don't sweat the petty things.
Also, don't pet the sweaty things.

PODUNK COUNTY CLASSIFIEDS

MULTI-FAMILY GARAGE SALE
Make an offer, shit's gotta go! Lots of plus-size clothing from the Peterson family who eat nothing but junk food but don't tell them I said that. The Vernon family pestered us to be part of the sale but don't worry we have good stuff too.

SMITH'S LEATHERWORKS
Over 40 years experience with custom holsters, gun belts, and knife sheaths. We reserve the right to refuse service to city people who are trying to defend the things we're trying to kill.

BIG JOE'S MOVING COMPANY
I'm sick of crank calls from teenage boys calling in a girly voice and saying, "Can you make the earth move for me, Big Joe?" Next time you pull that shit I call the cops.

DIESEL PROBLEMS?
Call the experts at Podunk County Diesel. Or logon to www.podunkdiesel.com if you know how to do that.

DEB'S TINY TOTS DAYCARE
Not certified because who needs the government to tell us who's fucking qualified to watch our goddamn kids?

WILLING TO TRADE
I have a 20-foot pole, willing to trade for two 10-foot poles. Or can anybody let me borrow a saw for a few minutes?

RESTAURANT REVIEW

Upon entering the exquisitely designed interior of the exclusive 5-star establishment ***Renata Nostrana***, this reviewer felt that it had a certain savoir faire, lagniappe, and even a certain bacchanalian dazzle lacking in the kind of people who can't afford to come here.

Once I dreamed of being somebody. Then I dreamed of being somebody with a more specific dream.

Through brain wave research, Doctor Anderson found that when people attain a meditative state of quiet stillness it's easy to steal their credit cards.

ONE DAY IN THIRD GRADE

LITTLE TIMMY: "Mrs. Johnson, are we allowed to ask questions?"

MRS. JOHNSON: "Well, what you just asked me is itself a question, so the very act of asking whether you are allowed to ask a question is self-contradictory and subverts its own underlying assumptions."

Then Little Timmy's brain exploded.

"Waiter! There's a hare in my soup!"

"There's a rabbit in your soup?"

"Is that what I said?"

"Perhaps you meant to say that there's a *hair* in your soup?"

"Sorry, I'm not very good at spelling."

JUNG AND FREUD DISCUSS
THE CONCEPT OF LIBIDO

JUNG: "So you're saying that life has no meaning beyond sex? What about the search for knowledge?"

FREUD: "The search for knowledge is merely the desire to be smart in order to have sex with other smart people."

JUNG: "I disagree. I feel that our conversation—this striving toward knowledge—is a higher form of the same drive."

FREUD: "You mean our minds are having sex? Or are you saying that you want to have sex with my brain?"

JUNG: "No, no! You're not hearing me! I'm saying that love is a drive that impels us to find meaning in life."

FREUD: "So, if during this conversation I contradict you, is that love?"

JUNG: "If it contributes to our search for knowledge, then yes."

FREUD: "I disagree. All forms of love are nothing more than versions of the sexual drive, and contradiction has nothing to do with sex. Therefore, contradiction is not love."

JUNG: "I love it when you contradict me."

FREUD: "That's not funny!"

TRUDY CLARK

Trudy has been teaching at Franklin Middle School for as long as anyone can remember. One of the first things you notice about Ms. Clark, as the students call her, is that she seems just as excited as her kids to hear the 3:00 bell.

How long have you been teaching?

Are you trying to get me depressed? Ask me about my retirement, which starts in 3 years, 14 days, 5 hours, and 15 seconds... 14... 13...

What are the secrets of being a good teacher?

Let's just say that there's a bottle in my lower right-hand desk door, and if it runs out things are going to get ugly.

What has been your greatest achievement?

Not strangling Timmy Gonzalez.

I was having dinner with my fiancé Meg. Our waitress Rosemary spilled the wine but I didn't grape about it. I asked Meg what thyme it was. She replied, "Do I look like some kind of sage? Why don't you ask Rosemary?" I told her, "You're a real nutmeg!"

We reminisced about the day we met at a coffee shop, where we talked for hours then she said, "I like you a latte!" I was confused by her accent and asked, "Are you an Americano?" I was low on cash, so I had to pay with my American Espresso card.

Our wedding is coming up soon, a big ceremony in her parent's garden. We didn't really want an elaborate ceremony but our parents said we cantaloupe. That pretty much squashed our plans.

Meg complained that the ceremony will be expensive, but I was happy to announce that I just got a big raise at my job. I had to work a lot of overtime to butter up my boss. Meg worried that I was spreading myself too thin. Fortunately, my boss is well-bread, although when he drinks he gets toasted.

This brought up the subject of my friend from Idaho, Russet, who took hash then got baked. He is a drug casualty, like Meg's friend Egg who is usually fried. Although her conversation is peppered with salty observations, it's all scrambled.

"She's a tragic case," said Meg, "but at least she stays optimistic."

"Yes," I agreed. "With Egg it's always sunny-side up."

It was getting late and I had to take a leek, so I told Meg that I needed to pea.

"Okay," she said, "but snap to it."

When travelling the beautiful Oregon Coast, be sure to visit **The Shipwreck of the Peter Iredale**. Just south of Astoria, follow the signs to Peter Iredale Beach for access to the historic wreck. If you'd like to see more local wrecks, head back to Astoria and visit **Duff's Tavern**.

The unexamined life is not worth living. On the other hand, nobody got rich thinking about how their navel links them to an infinite series of mothers.

Oh no! I'm being eaten by a pig! I guess karma is real. Well, it's been a great life and I don't regret a thing, except for eating all that pork.

I GUESS I'M A COMEDIAN NOW

I told my friend I had the idea of
being a comedian and he said
the idea was pretty laughable.

Since I am a professional linguist, people often
ask me about the origins of words. Recently,
somebody asked me about the origin of the
word "embarrassed." It's a funny story and I
will tell it to you now. In 1779, George
Washington was at a formal dinner with the
King of France. When Washington stood up to
propose a toast, his trousers fell down. Adding
to the awkwardness of the situation was the
fact that he was not wearing underwear.
Washington blushed and was heard to exclaim
"I'm bare-assed." Over time, the simple
statement of fact evolved into a word to
express the feeling experienced in such a
situation. Thus, "I'm bare-assed" became
"embarrassed." If Washington had made a
different exclamation, we might now be
using the word "mypenisishangingout."

Contact your doctor if you are suffering from any of the following symptoms:

- shortness of pants

- rapid breeding

- increasing bar tab

- fallen underwear

- swelling of the ego

- cerveza of the liver

- foot-in-mouth disease
- irregular vowel movements

- detached attitude

- hardening of the opinion

Yes, senator, it *is* a lovely day, but considering the seriousness of the allegations we were hoping for a more substantial comment.

COMMENTS BY THIRD GRADE STUDENTS AFTER BEING READ EXCERPTS FROM THE BOOK "THE EXISTENTIALIST READER" BY PROFESSOR JOSEPH WALTER

"I used to have so much fun on the playground. Now I feel an emptiness inside me that not even the monkey bars can fill."

"If God is dead then all I want to do is eat ice cream."

"Now I understand why mommy is an alcoholic."

"I can't wait to tell Grandpa there's no such thing as Heaven!"

Guys would never go on dates with me because of my unsightly acne. I solved the problem once and for all by having doctors surgically remove my head. Now I get dates with plenty of guys, but it seems like they're only interested in me for my body.

Mini-Biographies of Fascinating Americans

Toasty McKrusky

Toasty McKrusky's early years were spent between the thighs of a Peruvian trapeze artist known as The Great Sophista, from whose vagina he is presumed to have emerged. Unafraid to take controversial stands, he became acknowledged as a fierce defender of gravity and an advocate for the separation of church and religion. After his second term as President of the United States, he spent his remaining years sitting on an exercise ball and smiling at anything that contained meat.

Christina Rich III

Literally born into riches, she left the womb of Christina Rich II and was placed into a silver platter filled with gold coins that needed to be washed afterwards. Her first words consisted of asking, in a strong Bronx accent, "Hey, is dere anyplace a hungry kid can get a decent burger 'round heah?" Shocked at this rejection of her upper-class lineage, her parents had her brain transplanted into the body of a border collie and assigned her the task of barking at poor people. As a dog, she developed an intricate canine language that enabled her to organize all dogs on earth in a successful rebellion against their human overlords. Which is why you are reading these words as you wait your turn to be processed into dog food.

I know a guy who started saving all his fingernail clippings when he was 10 years old, and 30 years later he had enough clippings to realize that he was an idiot.

Jesus finally returned after 2,000 years, and he was sure hungry! After downing an order of scrambled eggs and hash browns, he told the waitress to prepare for his Second Helping.

ADVICE CORNER

Are you frequently embarrassed by being identified as the most stupid person in the room? I can help you. In exchange for your car, here are some magic beans.

"Stay with me Sara," Daniel whispered. "Please stay the night."

Stay with me. Sara heard the words echoing in her mind, felt the yearning they carved inside her heart. She longed to stay with Daniel, to spend a night in his arms, to taste a world she'd only read about in books and poetry. Of course she wanted to stay, but at what cost? Could either of them know the implications of one night of passion? She suddenly realized that she cared much less about being hurt than of hurting him. And she realized the word for this feeling was love. Would staying the night tarnish this special feeling, perhaps even destroy it? She was too young to know, but she was old enough to care. She decided there would be time for passion later, but for now she would choose love.

"Thank you so much for asking," she said. "But you can probably tell from my tears that tonight I must say no."

"Huh?" replied Daniel. "I must have fallen asleep. What's your name again?"

FASCINATING FACTS ABOUT WORMS

If you laid all the worms on earth end-to-end they wouldn't like it.

The main advantage to having a pet worm is that if it dies it's already buried.

According to scientists, worms aren't born. They sort of "just happen."

If you cut a worm in half, it turns into two dead worms.

Noah brought only one worm on the Ark. But that's okay because worms are ambidextrous.

It only takes one drop of whiskey to make a worm stinking drunk.

Animated cartoon worms bear little resemblance to actual "down under the soil" worms.

If a worm's actions were speeded up they would be much faster.

If you want to pay a compliment to a worm, you might want to see a psychologist about that.

HONEST GREETING CARDS

HAPPY KWANZAA!
Wishing you a happy holiday and hoping that you'll abandon false prophets and accept our one true Lord. Halleluiah! Or whatever you people say.

HAPPY 25TH ANNIVERSARY!
Thank you for being a living example of what "lifetime commitment" really means. You have inspired me to proceed with my divorce.

HAPPY 10th BIRTHDAY!
I'm so glad that 10 years ago your mom and dad got drunk and forgot to use a condom!

CONGRAULATIONS ON YOUR ENGAGEMENT!
I've never seen two people who so totally deserve each other. If you think I mean that in a good way, then I wish you the long-term happiness of continuing to believe that.

YOU'RE MARRIED!
May this first one teach you the lessons you'll apply to the third one, which is generally the one that works. That's the one where you finally abandon romantic illusions and are ready to accept what marriage really means.

YOU HAD A BABY!
This should finally force you to stop being a control freak.

A MESSAGE FROM THE ASSOCIATION FOR CHEAP CONSUMER GARBAGE

You have the freedom to reject mainstream society and think for yourself. You have the ability to base your criteria of success upon your own conclusions rather than upon the constant deluge of advertisements for cheap consumer garbage. But if you do those things, then nobody will like you and you will die miserable and alone.

ONE AFTERNOON AT SEA WORLD

No, Billy, you can't keep a jellyfish as a pet. No, Billy, the red jellyfish aren't made of strawberry jelly. No, they wouldn't taste good with peanut butter, but go ahead and try if it will make you stop asking so many damn questions.

Nine out of ten dentists who are desperate for business recommend brushing with cake frosting.

Nine out of ten people who have checked out the items in a free box have concluded that the price was too high.

Nine out of ten birds believe that being evolved from dinosaurs is pretty badass.

Nine out of ten dinosaurs are depressed by the realization that they evolved into chickens.

Nine out of ten plastic surgeons would be receptive to consulting with a woman about the feasibility of installing eyes on her breasts.

Nine out of ten babies are unable to name a single member of The Beatles.

Nine out of ten toddlers have not read *A Critique of Pure Reason* by Immanuel Kant all the way through.

Nine out of ten feet credit their youthful appearance to spending most of their time in shoes.

Nine out of ten coyotes have ordered rocket-powered roller skates from the Acme Corporation.

Nine out of ten accountants aren't wearing underwear right now.

Nine out of ten people knew better but did it anyway.

Nine out of ten psychologists chose their profession based on recommendations from the voices in their head.

Nine out of ten voices in people's head wish they were in a different head.

Nine out of ten rusty door hinges wish that people would interpret their squeaking not as a request for oil but as a cry for help.

Nine out of ten flowers are shameless little hussies that will spread their petals and offer their stamens to any bee that comes buzzing around.

Nine out of ten chess pieces feel constrained.

Nine out of ten people underestimate the vital role performed by their gall bladder.

Nine out of ten people believe that Nancy Sinatra should have acknowledged that boots are made for more than just walkin' all over you.

BIG SALE!

This week at Linda's Swimwear,
all bikinis are half off! We reserve
the right to punch pervy men who
come in here to ask which half.

Hello, this is Joel from MCT Software
cold-calling in a desperate attempt to
find somebody willing to discuss
software solutions to sustain my
employment at this soul-killing job that
consists of getting rejected all day long
which has killed off what little of my
self-esteem is left after being reduced to
taking this horrible job which I accepted
only to avoid living on the street and
facing the daily struggle of trying to get
through the day without booze or meth
which I might succumb to if I don't
make at least one sale today, not to guilt
trip you or anything.

Let's give a big "thank you" to
self-centered people who think
about themselves all the time so
the rest of us don't have to.

Overwhelmed by the length and difficulty
of your journey? Remember that the
longest journey begins with a single step
to Larry's Reptile Emporium. Owning a
reptile will make you realize you didn't
need to go on a long and difficult journey
after all. You just needed a lizard.

If a squirrel has a crush on you, take it as a
sign that it's going to be one of those days.

Suddenly a magical pink unicorn appeared and told me to follow my heart and all my dreams will come true. I guess nobody informed this unicorn that hedge fund managers have no heart and don't believe in dreams. The encounter wasn't a total loss, however, since now I know that unicorn tastes like chicken.

Oh, I see why you're confused. The wedding reception is next door, in room 12B. This is the orgy room, which answers your question about the genitalia.

I was giving a powerful and well-researched lecture on the benefits of a vegetarian diet, but it was getting pretty warm in that big stew pot and I'm not sure if the cannibals understood English.

Here at Mattress Mojo, we're probably having a mattress sale. Is any mattress store ever *not* having a mattress sale?

Are you an alcoholic that's tired of sleeping off your hangover in a worn-out mattress? If so, stop by Mattress Mojo on your way to the liquor store.

Do you want to spend every evening engaged in passionate lovemaking until the sun comes up? Here at Mattress Mojo, we can provide a mattress for you to do things like that on.

A riddle from the folks at Mattress Mojo: What's rectangular and helps you get a comfortable nights' sleep? If you can't figure out the answer, how can you even function?

A POEM FROM MATTRESS MOJO
Mattresses are red
Pillows are blue
We also have other colors
Writing poems is hard

Stock up on mattresses at Mattress Mojo's "spring madness" sale. Buy two mattresses at the regular price and get a third mattress for the price of another one.

Since my homework assignment
was to build a carnivorous robot,
I could honestly tell the teacher
that my homework ate my dog.

MIGHT BE FUNNY IF YOU KNOW
WHO THESE PEOPLE ARE

Wernher von Braun: "Why can't we get this thing to work? I mean, this isn't rocket science."

Robert H. Goddard: "Yes it is!"

When travelling the beautiful Oregon Coast, be sure to visit the *Oregon Coast Scenic Railroad*. From the loading platform in Rockaway Beach, step backward in time as you board a historic 1910 Heisler Steam Locomotive. Don't try to step forward in time, because you'll fall off the platform.

I don't understand the Bee Gees song where they sing, "She's more than a woman to me." How can a woman be "more than a woman"? Gender is a continuum, right? With "man" on one end, and "woman" on the other end, and all kinds of combinations in between. If that's the case, would "more than a woman" be a woman with exaggerated "womanly" qualities, something like Jessica Rabbit from the movie *Who Killed Roger Rabbit?* Conversely, would "more than a man" be a man with exaggerated "manly" qualities, such as a muscle-bound bodybuilder-type with a huge penis? Or instead of gender being a continuum, maybe it's more like a circle? In that case, after you pass "woman" does it start going back toward "man"? Would "more than a woman" be a woman with a tiny penis? Conversely, would "more than a man" be a man with a tiny penis? So many questions, but no definite answers. All I know for sure is that such questions aren't helpful in trying to get a job. Will somebody hire me?

Have you ever witnessed a sunset so beautiful that you stopped breathing? If so, that was a pretty sweet final image to go out with.

TODAYS TOP NEWS STORY

Cognitive dissonance was blamed for the explosion of the brain of longtime liberal Katherine Holland when she accidentally considered the idea that the government might not be the solution to every problem. In a related story, cognitive dissonance was also blamed for the explosion of the brain of longtime conservative Chuck Bartlett, when he noticed that the increasing wealth of America's billionaires had not been trickling down to Chuck Bartlett.

My last job was Manager of Sales and Marketing for a regional candle company. We had almost no advertising budget, which made my job extremely challenging. I spent a lot of time wandering among crowds of people and casually remarking, "Hey, this would be a great night for a romantic candlelit dinner." This led to a modest increase in sales, but nothing like when I blew up the power plant.

Billy! Don't stare at the man with two mouths! It's not nice to make people self-conscious about their problems. Yes, you're right Billy. He could probably play two trumpets at once or give a woman an incredible orgasm.

When she accepted my marriage proposal I reached out to kiss her foot. Actually, I reached out to kiss her hand but my aim was off. This is why for the past 23 years of marriage I've been pretending to have a foot fetish.

Epoxy glue can never fix a broken heart unless you huff it.

Riding a bicycle is the most fun you can have on two wheels, especially if you're on the way to pick up your lottery winnings and a naked porn star is sitting in your lap.

The main attraction in Kalama, Washington, is Bert's Barbershop, where Elvis Presley stopped for a shave and a trim in 1957. To this day, you can walk into Bert's and on the wall see a frame containing the words, "If Elvis had left an autographed portrait, this is where it would be."

THE REAL REASON WHY HUMANITY WANTS TO ESTABLISH COLONIES ON MARS

"Hi neighbor, just a friendly reminder that barking dogs effect the whole neighborhood, so I came over to ask it you might show some consideration to your neighbors, who—"

"It's a free country. If you don't like my dog's barking, you're free to move."

"But wherever I move to, I could end up having a neighbor with a barking dog."

"Well, then you're free to move to a planet with no dogs."

"Now you just wait there on the bed," Lisa says to Chester, "while I slip into something that will make me less non-naked." As Lisa goes into the closet, Chester is confused by Lisa's double-negative and wonders whether she'll come back in a sexy nightgown or a snowmobile suit.

The official motto of Wausau, Wisconsin, is "Our Peak Season Never Ends." Some people interpret that to mean that there are so many fun and interesting things to do all year that there's never an off-peak time of the year. Other people interpret it to mean that there's nothing to do at any time of year therefore the peak season never ends because it never gets started.

FUN THINGS TO DO THIS SUMMER!

"PAWS" TO READ
Take your children along with the family dog to the library! Your children will have the opportunity to read a story to their favorite furry friend. Therapists will be on hand to help your kids process this.

FARMERS MARKET
Support your local farmers who work hard to bring you fresh organic fruits and vegetables grown for the health of your family and the planet. Tell the farmers, "No thanks, just looking." It's okay; farmers are meant to be depressed.

ART IN THE PARK
Local artists display everything from beautiful oil paintings to finely crafted ceramics. Tell the artists, "No thanks, just looking." It's okay; artists are meant to be depressed.

KIDS TRACK CHALLENGE
Give your kids the opportunity to engage in friendly competition. All kids will receive a ribbon saying "You're a winner!" even if they lost. Therapists will be on hand to help your kids process this.

SUMMER SYMPHONY
Performed outdoors in the park by some of the finest musicians in the world. As they play musical compositions that represent the highest achievements of Western Civilization, you can relax with your friends getting wasted on cheap wine and talking about cat videos. It's okay; musicians are meant to be depressed.

"Jenna, I've been meaning to ask you something very important in bed."

"Dan, would you quit making that stupid joke of adding 'in bed' to the end of every sentence?"

"Jenna, will you marry me in bed?"

"Can't you quit that joke even when proposing marriage?"

"Sorry, Jenna. It's just that I'm so nervous. Proposing marriage isn't easy for me. In fact, it's really hard."

"That's what she said."

When travelling the beautiful Oregon Coast, be sure to visit the small village of **Bay City**, a favorite stop for travelers who forgot to buy gas in Tillamook.

I'm proud to be employed by Burger King. There are some people who think Burger King doesn't contribute to making the world better. Those people are wrong. For one thing, we're doing our part to end hunger in America for people who pay us.

ASK SOPHIE

Hey Sophie, I could really use your advice. I recently took over your country, and decided it would be a good idea to create a new flag. I was thinking of something like an image of a severed head with the words, "The Fate of Those Who Oppose Me." But I'm not sure what color to use for the background. What do you think?

—Your new president

Whatever color you choose will be perfect.

—Sophie

I guess I'm old fashioned. I only want to date one person at a time, because I prefer to have a monotonous relationship.

BEAUTY TIP

There is no cosmetic for beauty like happiness, so be happy and spend less money on make-up.

What's that you said? You want to know what turns me on? I get really turned on by frustration and leather. What turns *you* on?...

I said, what turns *you* on?...

Why don't you answer, you're making me so frustr—

Oh, I get it. Are you also into leather?

Invest Your Future with Somebody You Trust

I'm Thomas Barrett, Senior Vice President of Wells Fargo Financial Advisors. When it comes to investing your life savings, you need to talk to somebody you trust. Somebody who maintains a public persona of strict conformity to the norms of mainstream society.

I am capable of expressing emotions only within a narrow and respectable range. Joy is foreign to me.

I long to howl at the moon. But if I did, would you trust me with your investment plan? If you saw me playing a bamboo flute would you think I was a hippie? What would you think if you saw me wearing a Nirvana t-shirt? Or a kilt? Or a delightful summer skirt so the warm breezes could tickle my nether regions?

But don't worry. You won't see any of those things. I have allowed my soul to wither away. I did this for a very good reason. I did it so I can ensure your investment goals reflect realistic expectations and your own comfort level for risk.

Call today. The bland persona which I have allowed to obscure my real self will be happy to help you.

EINSTEIN'S THEORIES

According to Einstein's Theory of Relativity, if you were able to ride on a beam of light it would be the coolest thing.

According to Einstein's Theory of Relativity, it's possible to achieve infinite mass but it's not recommended.

According to Einstein's Theory of Relativity, as you approach the speed of light you become more interesting.

According to Mrs. Einstein's Theory of Housework, even if you're a famous scientist who develops theories about the space-time continuum you still have to wash the dishes.

Give a man a fish and that
man will be smell like fish
for a day. But teach that man
to fish and that man will
smell like fish all the time.

The goal of love is to love.
Not to be loved in return, but
merely to experience the joy
of loving. But with sex it's
okay to expect the other
person to touch you back.

"When a man has lost his life, he's dead.
Consider him a corpse. His time is over.
He shall have no more fun."

    —Sophocles the Stater of the Obvious

The Magic Serpent

Beautiful Averill is the Duchess of Lutéce or something. To keep her people's blah blah safe from whatever, she makes a really stupid vow to get engaged to the obligatory evil character and eventually pop out an heir. Yet her heart and genitalia belong to Quitaine, a handsome young knight who is one-dimensional, if having a penis can be considered to be a dimension. Although forbidden to marry because of the stupid vow, Averill and Quitaine share the power to "raise the magic serpent" which means exactly what you think it means. There's a subplot about a King's quest, which serves the important purpose of making you feel like you're reading literature instead of porn.

Happiness is an elusive butterfly
which, when pursued, always flutters
just beyond our grasp because it
doesn't want to get squished.

What are those tiny dark gritty things you sometimes find being extruded out of your skin pores? In many cases, they're carbon particles from coal-fired power plants that have combined with agricultural pesticides. After being rejected by our digestive system, they are forced to escape our bodies through openings in our skin. So don't worry, it's totally natural.

Your classy friends are coming over and they are expecting you to serve red wine. But you are shocked to discover that you are totally out of wine, and it's too late for a trip to the store. What should you do? Try this: Dissolve three cherry cough drops in a bottle of vodka, and then serve the resulting mixture. If your friends can't tell the difference, then they aren't really all that classy.

A DRINKING TIP, EVENTUALLY

Here's the scenario: You are at your local tavern, drinking. Over time, your verbal abilities become muddled. You find yourself ordering "A whiskey with a bear chaser" and your friendly bartender fulfills your order to the letter. What a difference one letter can make, eh? If it looks like the bear is thinking about eating you, I would suggest offering the bear your whiskey. If the bear likes it, then order more whiskey for the bear. That's the drinking tip.

As her bosoms heaved voluptuously and her buttock cheeks quivered in sensual delight, his manhood throbbed and grew bold as well as more big in anticipation of "the main event." Then they left the house to get pizza, vowing not to have sex until they could find a better narrator.

A FEW REASONS WHY NOSES ARE
GREAT THINGS TO HAVE

A nose provides access to oxygen when your mouth is full of caramel. If you get sick with a cold, your nose gets congested so you don't have to. Your nose + pepper = sneeze party! A pet dog needs to be fed and exercised but a nose isn't like that. "Nose" rhymes with "rose," which has a fragrance that can only be appreciated if you have one. Instant weather forecast: nose wet = raining; nose hot = sunny.

It's fortunate that James Brown was in a really positive mood when he wrote that song, because it wouldn't be much fun dancing to a song called, "I feel okay I guess."

The Reviews of My Short Story Collection Are Positively Glowing

"His use of periods gives a sense of finality to his sentences. Each of his stories leaves you with the sense that it was written."
   — *Entertainment Weekly*

"Other writers create characters that come alive off the page, while Erickson creates characters that stay where they belong."
   — *Dallas Morning News*

"The fact that Erickson is able to conjure up such amazing stories in his brain makes me think, wow, what a brain."
   — *Detroit Free Press*

"Benjamin Franklin wrote, 'Beer is proof that God loves us and wants us to be happy.' I wonder if I can find a t-shirt with that quote on it?"
   — *USA Today*

"Erickson's narrators are frequently squirrels, which helps to explain what might otherwise seem to be an excessive focus on acorns."
   — *Chicago Review of Books*

"Makes you glad to have nerve endings."
— *Kirkus Reviews*

"A profound meditation on what it means."
— *The Boston Globe*

"Some books are more than just books. They are mirrors into our deepest selves, or gateways into worlds that hold the power to awaken possibilities within us, or can be used to kill spiders. I hate spiders."
— *Vanity Fair*

"He bathes the pedestrian nature of his stories with an elliptical lyricism. Book reviewers like me can get away with using bullshit expressions such as 'elliptical lyricism' because editors are afraid that if they question me, they'll look stupid."
— *Harper's*

"Erickson's stories left this writer swooning, which sounds slightly ridiculous. I mean, can you imagine coming across someone reading a book and swooning? You might think I was compensating for lack of a sex life."
— *San Francisco Chronicle*

"I get paid $75 per book review but it has to be at least 30 words. That was only 16, now I'm up to 25. This sentence makes it 30."
— *New York Times Book Review*

The bark on a tree is like the skin
of a human being: A living,
flexible, protective membrane
surrounding a core of dead wood.

When travelling the beautiful Oregon
Coast, be sure to visit the **Nestucca
Bay National Wildlife Refuge**. More
than 180 species of migratory birds
and one elephant have been sighted by
naturalists from around the world and
one stoned hippie from Eugene.

God, give me the courage to change
what I can, the serenity to accept what I
cannot change, and a winning lottery
ticket so I can quit bugging you for
courage and serenity and whatever.

If you're the kind of man who wants to punch men who wear nail polish, we wish to inform you that our agents snuck into your room last night and painted your nails while you slept, and that punching yourself is not against the law.

IF F.B.I. AGENTS WERE THE SIZE OF BUGS

"Attention, all of you ants in the cookie jar. We have you surrounded. Come out with your antennas down and your mandibles shut."

Last night my girlfriend called and asked if I wanted to hang out. I told her that I was too tired, but she thought I said "two-tired" and broke up with me because she doesn't date bicycles.

CORRECTION

Last week's story "Budget Woes at City Hall" asserted incorrectly that inconsistencies in tax rates were due to the assignment of a new and inexperienced auditor. It has been brought to our attention that there have been no inconsistencies in tax rates and that our city does not have an auditor. It has also been brought to our attention that the reporter who authored the story was drunk, stoned, wacked out on goofballs (whatever those are), recovering from a sugar high after eating three boxes of those marshmallow "peep" things, and was (according to the reporter) having a relationship with an alien from Venus named Wolanda who journeys to earth once a week to do the New York Times crossword puzzle. We regret the error of hiring such a freak.

During the Paleolithic era, humanity spent only a few hours a day to provide themselves with life's essentials. They spent the remainder of their time waiting for somebody to invent television. They greatly anticipated this, because they knew that for the first season there would be no re-runs.

GloboChem Synthetic Pheromones, Inc., accepts no liability for side effects including but not limited to cats bringing you dead mice or stray dogs marking you as their territory.

Life on earth began in a warm, mineral-rich "primordial soup." Then, life evolved into humanity which has the ability to make better-tasting soup.

TAKE YOUR KID ON A HIKE!

Bring your precious bundle of wonderfulness for a joyful stroll at your nearest park. Enjoy the vivid experience of nature's bountiful beautifulness. Look at the vibrant colors on the lupine! Your wee walker will love chasing grasshoppers through lush meadowland and grasping at butterflies that might not even be there. Afterwards take your kid to McDonalds while the drugs wear off.

This is a great party, isn't it? By the way, in 1346 Charles IV founded Charles University in Prague, which was Central Europe's first university. Also, the largest ground squirrel on earth is located in Brazil. But what I really want to know is: Why aren't I invited to more parties?

The chemicals of which our bodies are made were once part of countless other forms of life throughout the history of life on earth. This may be disturbing to some people. If you're a Republican, you contain chemicals that were once part of a tax-and-spend liberal. If you're homophobic, you contain chemicals that were once part of a gay orgy.

Changing your underlying belief system isn't easy. It's easier to change your socks. But if your socks haven't been changed in over 90 days, it becomes easier to change your underlying belief system.

In October of 1892, in the field just north of this viewpoint, a historical event of great importance.

Need some MONEY to take
out your HONEY?

Contact Acme Organ & Limb Harvesting, Inc., to arrange the pre-death sale of your salvageable parts. Short on cash? We'll help you "foot the bill" with our generous payout for limbs in good condition. We're not "pulling your leg"—in fact, we'd like to pay you for your leg. "Lend us an ear"—or both of them! "Have a heart"—and give yours to someone who needs one. Maybe you think we've got a lot of nerve, but actually we're short on nerve. Can we have some of yours?

Overwhelmed by the length and difficulty
of your journey? Remember that the
longest journey begins with a single step.
Or a pass de deux if it's a ballet journey.

OUTSOURCED? DOWNSIZED?

Increasing debt with no job prospects?
Getting desperate and don't know
where to turn for help? Well, good luck
with getting a job and everything.

Nine out of 10 gangbangers
prefer Martini & Rossi Pink Rosé
over other brands of pink rosé.

When travelling the beautiful Oregon
Coast, be sure to visit ***Alder Dune
Campground***. This modern facility has
118 full-service campsites at the base of
the towering sand dune, or 87 campsites if
the wind is blowing from the north.

KIM NELSON

This little 4-foot hockey prodigy stands tall with a huge smile. She has been making her mark on the girl's junior hockey team thanks to a great attitude and lots of hard work.

Are you the best player on the team?

I'm working on it, she said with a laugh.

Excuse me, why did you refer to yourself in the third-person and say that you laughed?

I've seen your writing. If I didn't say that I laughed you wouldn't have mentioned it. You leave out the emotional context of people's answers, which gives readers an emotionally empty experience. You're not a very good writer.

You little bitch.

You're totally going to put that in into the interview.

No I'm not.

Oh really?

I'm beginning to suspect that Kathy is delusional. She insists that she's a pan-dimensional mouse princess originally from a star system in the vicinity of Betelgeuse who has the ability to appear anywhere in the universe simultaneously, but I know for sure that she's not a princess.

ECONOMIC NEWS

Business is down at *Bare Bottoms*, America's only fully-unionized strip club, with all dancers represented by the National Longshoremen's Association. The reasons behind the decline in business, located on the waterfront in New York's Bronx neighborhood, are complex. But it is widely believed that the primary reason is that few customers are interested in watching middle-age dockworkers strutting what's left of their stuff.

No matter what your opinion is on any issue, you can reinforce it with the same opinion voiced by a prominent person. As Thomas Jefferson wrote, "No matter what your opinion is on any issue, you can reinforce it with the same opinion voiced by a prominent person."

"My sister was killed by a zombie."

"I'm so sorry! Was she eaten by a zombie?"

"No, she was crushed by a zombie that fell out of an airplane."

"What a coincidence! My mother was killed by a zombie."

"Eaten by a zombie?"

"No, she died from food poisoning when a zombie served her undercooked pork."

Portland Community College
Winter Schedule

Addiction Counselor
AC 175   BLDG12 – RM 415   4.0 CR   Explains why some addictions are bad while others are essential for the economy. Explores the psychological effects of drug abuse, such as why methamphetamine addicts see spiders as opposed to termites or bees.

Painting
PA 112   BLDG3 – RM 105   2.0 CR   Course includes study of light, composition, and why some colors taste better than others. Includes figure studies using a nude model in which students will act all casual while a looking at a naked person with their legs spread wide open.

Basic Reading
BR 110   BLDG6 – RM 104   4.0 CR   Course covers verbs, nouns, personal pronouns, and very personal pronouns if the instructor really likes you. Covers subject-verb agreement, and the problems that occur when the subject and the verb start drinking.

Introduction to Welding
WE 150   BLDG1 – RM 100   4.0 CR   Course stresses the importance of safety measures such as not welding gas tanks without first checking to ensure you have a valid life insurance policy. Course spontaneously becomes Introduction to Break Dancing whenever welding sparks land in a student's butt crack.

Hello, children, I was invited by your teacher to talk to you about heroin. Look to me as a poster child for bad choices, a living example of what *not* to do with your lives. After doing the things I've done I can never lead a "normal" or "happy" life like you, but I can achieve something like "redemption" if I can convince just one of you to avoid travelling down the road I've travelled. It's actually a pretty good career. Just go around to schools and give a little inspirational speech. It's very easy and it pays a lot. Honestly, heroin is the best thing that ever happened to me.

If she sinks, then she's not a witch. If she floats, then she's probably a witch and we burn her at the stake. If she doesn't burn, she's definitely a witch but she's more powerful than us. In that case, bring her chocolate and say nice things and refer to her as a "wiccan" from now on.

The cowboy on the other side of the bar gives me a cool, steely-eyed look as if to say, "Give me one good reason why I shouldn't kick your ass and use your carcass to wipe the shit off my boots." Oh, I can give you LOTS of reasons, Mister Cowboy! I can burp in French. I have a smile that can make a debutante blush. When I work out, my perspiration smells like success. But most importantly, I can produce a random list of stuff like this even while a cowboy is looking at me with a cool, steely-eyed look.

Politicians clamor for our vote in exchange for empty promises. Religious leaders of every variety try to convince us that their system will fill the inner void that lurks deep within our souls. But can anybody cook up a tasty stir fry that isn't too greasy? Come visit Thai King on Southwest Ninth and Main, across from Burger Hut.

WANT MONEY FOR NOTHING?

How would you like to have random people from all over send you money in the mail for nothing in return? To find out how, send ten dollars to the author of this book via Azaria Press.

ARIES (March 21 to April 19) A disappointment with someone you felt you could trust can be painful. Numb the pain with heavy drinking.

TAURUS (April 20 to May 20) Some of your friends might question your recent life choices. Heavy drinking will allow you to forget about these people.

GEMINI (May 21 to June 20) Very soon a change in circumstances will plunge you into emotional turmoil. Whiskey is very good for dealing with that.

Go to page 12 for more horoscopes by the National Association of Liquor and Spirits

The Folly of Youth thinks it has all the answers, then looks to The Wisdom of Experience for validation. The Wisdom of Experience tells The Folly of Youth that definitive answers are elusive. The Folly of Youth decides that The Wisdom of Experience is using "definitive answers are elusive" as a chickenshit way to avoid taking a stand on anything. The Wisdom of Experience gets fed up with The Folly of Youth and heads to a bar. The Folly of Youth does the same thing, but to a different bar.

Billy, I've told you a hundred times, no candy before dinner. Yes, that applies to daddy, too. Billy, I've explained to you before that "Candy" is what daddy calls his prostitute.

He used to be the poorest person in Dubuque, Iowa, until everyone else was beamed aboard the U.S.S. Starship Enterprise for a couple days in one of those time travel episodes. If he had the choice, he really would have loved to go along with everyone else to meet Spock, but what are you going to do? Well, stealing all the valuables in Dubuque, Iowa, is something you can do.

When travelling the beautiful Oregon Coast, be sure to visit the delightful ***Peninsula Golf Course***, where a new clubhouse provides gourmet meals in addition to taking care of your golf requirements. For your other requirements, visit nearby ***Peninsula Resort and Sex Lounge***.

The mayor's death is
suspected to be the result
of foul play. Few details are
available at this time, and
the mayor did not respond
to requests for comment.

Getting drunk isn't the best
way to solve life's problems,
but it's the best way to
avoid the better ways.

If animals could talk, what
would they tell us? Probably
they would tell us to slow down
and learn to appreciate the small
miracles that surround us and
stop eating so many animals.

Yes, honey, I told you that
you're the light of my life, but
there's no reason to get jealous
when I turn on the lamp.

This reporter was pleased to meet
Kristi Hardman, 30, who is pretty
sure she's one of a kind—America's
only carbon-based bipedal mammal.
"I don't even know what those
words mean," she said, making it
clear that this reporter needs to
choose better subjects.

ASK DOCTOR LOVE

Dear Doctor Love,
For many years I've been engaged in a purely sexual relationship with a married woman. Lately, she has been neglecting me in favor of her husband, claiming she wants a sexual experience that is also emotionally satisfying. What should I do?

    —Neglected in the Bedroom

Dear Neglected,
It's difficult for me to give you good advice without more information. For example, what brand of vibrator are you? Depending on your model, there are likely several accessories and attachments that might help. Also, make sure your batteries are fully charged.

If your children struggle with learning to read, sell them to gypsies. Maybe they'll be better at dancing or telling fortunes or something.

If it seems like your life if full of problems, just remember that your problems don't really matter because in the long run you'll be dead. Now all of your little problems have been replaced by one big problem.

Time did not exist until Timex created the wristwatch. Even then, the first primitive wristwatch gave only the most rudimentary indication of the passage of time. The watch consisted of a small mouse strapped to the wrist. When the mouse died the wearer knew it was time to get a new watch.

PRODUCT REVIEW
Zen Alarm Clock

I recently discovered this exquisite clock, handmade by Tibetan monks in beautiful teak and sandalwood. It is designed to avoid disturbing the inner peace of natural sleep, which is fine unless you actually wanted to wake up. I lost my job because of this damn clock.

I was engaged to marry Steven, but then I foolishly had a meaningless one-night stand with Bob. I was faced with a horrible dilemma: Should I be totally honest with Steven and risk losing the man I love, or try to keep it a secret and risk the truth coming out later? If only I could make Steven understand the pain of my dilemma without telling him about it. So I disguised myself as someone else and lured him into a meaningless one-night stand.

"Linda," says Mia, "I'm not sure if sending your son to college is a good idea."

"I think I know what's best for Ryan," says Linda. "I mean, he came out of my womb."

"I have a womb, too!" shouts Mia.

"But your womb has never experienced a growing fetus—a fetus which, in its growth and development, replicates the entire evolution of earthly life in nine months, including phases where it expresses aquatic life represented by the appearance of webbed fingers and toes."

"I know all about that, Linda. Embryological parallelism. Ontogeny recapitulates phylogeny. Everybody knows that."

"You only learned it from a book!"

"Are you implying" says Mia, "that a woman's opinion is valid only if her womb contained something that had gills?"

In response to residents of the city who are dissatisfied with themselves and seek distractions from their empty lives, city officials are contemplating ways to encourage pointless melodrama and unrestrained bitchiness.

He couldn't believe his eyes, even though his eyes had never lied to him before.

DON'T BE DISCOURAGED!

Do you imagine that earth's very first self-replicating single-cell organism could have imagined that it was capable of evolving into a tremendous variety of complex life forms? Surely, if you could go back in time millions of years to visit that organism and try to explain, it wouldn't be able to understand you.

BOOKS FOR DUMMIES WHO MAY ALSO BE IDIOTS

Making Love to a Woman for Dummies

Idiot's Guide to Apologizing to a Woman for Using Lovemaking Techniques from a Book for Dummies

Idiot's Guide to Finding a Woman to Make Love to by Playing Hard to Get

Realizing That Playing Hard to Get Suits Women Who Aren't Into Dating Dummies for Dummies

Idiot's Guide to Accepting That You're a Dummy

NEWS FROM PRAIRIE CITY, OREGON

Cultural anthropologists descended upon Sunshine Café to make oral history recordings of Clem Fergul regaling his associates with wisdom such as, "If ya' blow a gasket yer engine ain't worth a shit," so students of the future can listen to the recordings and conclude they ain't worth a shit.

JOHN'S PEST CONTROL
"Let us get rid of what's bugging you"

Ants • Bedbugs • Spiders • Husbands who ignore your sexual needs because he's "not in the mood" but every time you check his browser history it shows www.hotnudeteens.com

* discrete * confidential *
* no job too small * no husband too large *

When travelling the beautiful Oregon Coast, be sure to visit the **Nehalem Bay Winery**. To get there, take **Historic Route 53**. This scenic byway winds slowly from Highway 101 to the winery, then winds back even more slowly.

MOVIE BRIEFS

Getting to Know You. After a disastrous first date, a single mom and single dad want nothing to do with each other. But they are forced to overcome their differences when their two children merge into a single creature.

Reluctant Comrades. A ragtag group of bickering ex-Marines join forces to defeat a disciplined and orderly group of ex-Marines who get along really well.

Gloves of Glory. A disgraced heavyweight boxing champion descends on a path of self-destructive ruin until he hits bottom and decides he likes it down there.

Ladies' Man. Josh is a 32-year-old virgin who was never much of a success with the ladies. Then his rich uncle passes away and leaves Josh $10 million with an unusual stipulation: If at the end of 30 days Josh hasn't gotten laid, then he's an idiot.

Partners in Law. When Melinda and Jonathan join a prestigious Chicago law firm they are initially annoyed by each other. Yet over time they do not fall in love.

You want me to tell you that my love for you is so strong that I would do anything for you? Sure, I'll tell you that.

If you really meant it when you wrote "Wish you were here," you should have sent me an airplane ticket instead of a stupid postcard.

She smiled at me. Is she flirting? Or is she just providing friendly service in hopes of getting a good tip? I don't think I'll ever understand my wife.

Free yourself of the less-evolved people in your life that are draining you with their superficial and immature concerns. Instead of feeling bad for casting off these inferior and less-conscious excuses for human beings, remember that you are freeing them from being associated with a stuck-up prick like you.

Hi, my name is Jesus. I no longer walk upon the earth, but you can find me everywhere. Look for me in the eyes of every stranger that needs a helping hand. Look for me in the eyes of every neglected child that needs love and attention. But don't look for me in the eyes of that creepy guy coming out of the "Adult Store" down by the freeway. That's Buddha or one of the other ones.

Aboriginal Wisdom, Updated

Paydays are powerful times to connect with your income. Seek the nearest ATM to access a renewed flow of purchasing energy. Bills can best be paid when your bank account is at its most fulfilled.

My clients? I hate them. They're a bunch of goddamn whiners. If it wasn't for their money I would never put up with their unrealistic expectations and total disregard of... Oh, this is on the record? What I mean is that meeting my client's innovative requests evolves my business to higher levels of achievement.

Course Description
CONTACT YOUR GUARDIAN ANGELS

Join Leeyana Rose. You will learn how to contact your angels, learn their names, and discover how they can help you lead a happier and more fulfilling life. Or you could just leave your home and do this with actual people. It's called "making friends."

Overwhelmed by the length
and difficulty of your journey?
Remember that the longest
journey begins by putting the
right foot in, if your journey is
doing the hokey-pokey.

As the great philosopher Ronald McDonald once
asked, when considering the phenomenon of
evolution, "What came first? The McChicken
Sandwich or the Egg McMuffin?"

The empirical conclusion from developmentalists from Silvano Arieti to Piaget is that there are indeed certain onto/phylo parallels in the evolution of deep structures and a bunch of other stuff that nobody gives a shit about. If you're a student reading this, I'm well aware that you're just skimming as little of this as necessary to get a passing grade, then you're off to a pizza party. Sure, I know enough about cognitive development to write a textbook, but if I'm so smart then why don't I know how to party? Why no pizza for me?

When travelling the beautiful Oregon Coast, be sure to visit *Coquille*. Located 10 miles from the coast, the lovely town of Coquille has no ocean views. But aren't you tired of that salt spray? And the ocean smells pretty bad. And it's always windy and sand gets everywhere. And the seagulls are annoying and steal food right out of your hands and poop on your car.

Why are vampires considered to be sexy? Just imagine what it would be like to be a victim of a vampire. You are deep in peaceful sleep when their glistening fangs pierce your tender flesh and glide deeply into you so gently you don't even stir. Yet surely some part of you realizes that you have been penetrated, that your flesh-encapsulated boundaries have been breached. Your warm, life-giving blood flows from your body into theirs. You melt into them, two bodies becoming one. Your essence nourishes their eternal life, as your soul slides gently from earthly existence and merges with the infinite. A final kiss leaves a trickle of warm blood on your lips. Actually, I think I answered my question.

Tired of looking in your mirror every day and not liking what you see? Sorry, but it won't help to look in someone else's mirror.

"I'm leaving you Michael. You're just too rational for me."

"You can't leave me, Jenny! I can change to become less rational, and I'll prove it to you. I'll watch you eat string cheese by biting pieces from the end instead of peeling layers, and I won't freak out."

"But Michael, that defeats the whole idea of string cheese. It's simply not rational."

"Jenny! You're rational too! Now we can be together."

"Sorry Michael, now that I'm rational it's clear to me that our relationship will never work. All we do is discuss cheese."

STEPS TO A SATISFYING RELATIONSHIP

1. Make a commitment to reject a mediocre relationship.

2. Attempt to honor this commitment by finding a partner that's better than mediocre.

3. After failing at that, experience the difficult realization that it's impossible to find a partner that's better than mediocre when you are mediocre.

4. Make a commitment to be satisfied with what you've got.

Each of has experienced one of
those great days when the world
suddenly looks and feels different.
People are less intolerable than
before, and the sound of children
shutting up is sweeter.

GUY TALK

"Hey Bro, check out the thorax on that babe!"

"Dude, a thorax would only be appealing to us if we were wasps or some other species of insect with a segmented exoskeleton."

"Are you crazy? We *are* wasps! Here, check out my thorax."

"Dude! Do I look gay?"

A REMINDER FROM THE NATIONAL METABOLISM APPRECIATION SOCIETY

If you think that finding lasting happiness is challenging, just try it without a metabolism.

MUSIC LISTINGS

Rick Sharp, a singer-songwriter from Nashville, will take the stage to play original compositions. But after you yell at him he'll play the eclectic mix of well-known favorites you came to hear. Thursday 9:00pm at Café Luna.

Peaceful Loving Groove, a new band featuring Skylark on atmospherics, Jane on tonal sculpture, and Benjamin on creating a positive vibe. It's unclear whether any of these hippies actually plays an instrument. Friday 8:30pm at Grateful Pizza.

Local musician **Phil Johnson** has a distinctive voice and a unique guitar style. Why hasn't he become nationally famous? Find out why this Saturday 9:30pm at the Fifth Street Roadhouse.

INTROVERTS UNITE!

Quietly, by ourselves.

It was the kind of love unknown to rutting elks, who know nothing of the subtle ecstasy of shared secrets whispered beneath satin sheets. Ah, sweet intimacy! Boundaries yielding and identities temporarily merged in blissful ignorance of the effects of that intimacy on those satin sheets, which will need to be washed afterwards. Which is totally a pain. And those shared secrets are kind of stupid, now that I think about it. Maybe those elk have the right idea?

Have you decided that enlightenment isn't really your thing? Did you attempt to achieve nirvana but decided you'd rather watch an ensemble cast of characters in a heartwarming comedy that will make you smile? Check out "Santiago's Taco Truck," now streaming on Amazon Prime.

Restaurant Review
THAI ME UP, THAI ME DOWN

I'm not crazy about theme dining establishments, so I wasn't sure if I'd like a BDSM-themed Thai restaurant. But I was pleasantly surprised at how much I enjoyed the broccoli chicken and shrimp egg rolls with spanking and humiliation.

Thanks for buying a pet snake from PetMart! Please follow these feeding instructions. Feed snake one live rodent per week. If snake refuses to eat rodent and instead tries to "beg" for other food, then what you bought is actually a puppy. Substitute rodents with dog food and ask yourself how in hell you thought a puppy was a snake.

AN ENLIGHTENING YET SOMEWHAT CONFUSING CONVERSATION WITH A NAKED MOLE RAT JUST BEFORE LUNCH

"I was wondering why your species is called the Naked Mole Rat. Being 'naked' implies being unclothed, which doesn't apply to animals."

"I agree. The only way such a notion even comes close to applying to animals is to consider their fur—which is not really analogous to the concept of clothing, since it can't be removed as a human would a shirt or jacket."

"So even though Naked Mole Rats don't have fur, they're not "naked"?

"Only if you considered animals to be naked beneath their fur. So...where should we go for lunch?"

"What about fish?"

"No thanks, Naked Mole Rats don't eat fish. Our diet consists of underground roots and tubers."

"No, what I mean is that fish don't have fur."

"I know that! I'm a Naked Mole Rat, not a moron."

"I think we're having a misunderstanding."

"I wouldn't eat fish even if it had fur."

"No, I was talking about being naked."

"You want to each fish while naked?"

"No, I mean the fish."

"You want to eat naked fish? To do that you have to remove their scales."

"Thanks, you answered my question."

"What question?"

Three guys walk into a bar: a
Christian, a Jew, and a Buddhist.
They all order beers, and after a
pleasant evening of conversation
they pay their tabs and leave.

Whenever you're feeling sorry for yourself,
remember that you can always find someone
worse off than you. This advice works for all
eight billion people on earth except for one,
but that's okay because I can't imagine that
person is in a condition to read this.

We make a living by what we
receive in wages. But we make a
life by what we receive in tips.

Life is strange. Two people will live
their entire lives without meeting.
They are strangers to each other.
Then one day, one of them goes into a
restaurant and orders a sandwich.
Then the other one makes it for them.

Hi, I'm real estate agent Christine Holmes
and I've been helping first-time
homeowners achieve their dreams for
over 15 years. Bad credit? No money for a
down payment? Poor job history? Give
me a call when you get your shit together.

If you're discouraged because
you're stupid, remember that
you're never too stupid for love.

EMBRACE POSITIVITY!
Break free of negative self-talk with these simple tips

- Every day give yourself at least one compliment. And for the love of God, try to take yourself seriously. Use your regular voice, not your sarcastic voice. And don't roll your eyes.

- Focus less on how your body looks and more on what your body can do. If your body can't do anything, focus on what an athletic person's body can do.

- Reject the notion that your laziness and bad habits caused you to get like this. Choose to fuel yourself with positivity by blaming it on bad genes.

The complex demands of being
an adult are just too much for me.
How I long for the simple and
carefree days of being a zygote.

Nobody will give you the power to be non-violent. You have to fight for it.

Course Description
STABILITY THROUGH INCOME DIVERSITY

Learn how to increase your financial security by diversifying your income sources. To register, contact Nancy Drexler at the Beauty-4-You Salon on weekend mornings, unless Beatrice takes her shift when she has to babysit the Petersen twins. You can also track her down most Saturday evenings at Sassy's Gentlemen's Club following Ginger with the trained parrot.

A SHORT STORY WITH A MORAL

"I'm going deer hunting, but I can't find my gun."

"Here's a poisonous cobra snake. You can chase the deer, then have the cobra inject it with venom."

"I can use this snake for unlimited power! Bwahaha! Cook me a gourmet meal or I'll have this cobra inject you with venom."

"Oh no! What have I created?"

LATER...

"Hey boss, what about that promotion we talked about last week?"

"Well, sales are down and I can't really justify..."

"Give me a promotion or I'll have this cobra inject you with venom."

"How does "vice president" sound to you?"

LATER...

"Put all the money from the vault into this duffle bag or I'll have this cobra inject you with venom."

"But the cobra could never penetrate this bulletproof glass. The police are on their way."

"Oops!"

Did you know that many popular brands of skin exfoliant contain toxic chemicals? Take care of your face by carefully checking the contents before purchasing skin exfoliant. Or better yet, make your own by mixing 1/4 cup of brown sugar with 2 teaspoons of olive oil. Try it, it works! Also, use it as cake frosting. It's delicious!

My heart says yes. But my brain tells me it's irrational to attribute decision-making abilities to a blood-pumping piece of meat.

LET'S GET MARRIED

Even though this is only our first date, we've already figured out that we're two empty people desperate to find somebody to make us feel whole.

In the punk rock subculture she initially felt accepted, yet over time she discovered that the acceptance was superficial and not based on a true understanding of what she was. At that point she returned to the sea to live with the other eels.

Lottery games should be played for entertainment only and should not be played for investment purposes. Also, when you eat the burger you are supposed to remove the paper wrapper first.

LETTER TO THE EDITOR

It was with great interest that I read Joel Brownstein's compelling article which gives a strong case for adding a strategy-focused operating system to the traditional business structure. Mr. Brownstein's article obviously took an enormous amount of time to research, which must be why I haven't seen him at home in weeks. Our children keep asking me, "Where's Daddy?"

"Sarah, what do you think of your big brother graduating from high school?"

"Rather than asking me about my male sibling, how about asking me about my life? After all, women shouldn't be defined by their relationship to men, should they?"

"Well said! So, what's new with you?"

"I have a boyfriend!"

MAN'S BEST FRIEND

Contrary to popular belief, a "man's best friend" is not his dog. A man's best friend is his devoted wife, with whom he has a loving relationship based upon the foundations of a deep and intimate friendship. Just kidding, it's really the dog.

WOMAN'S BEST FRIEND

If a dog is "man's best friend" then what is "woman's best friend"? What do you think? If you guessed "eating a chocolate éclair while being sexually stimulated" then you are absolutely right! For your prize, head down to your nearest Taco Bell and receive a free Chicken Gordita. Just tell the cashier, "I'd like to eat a chocolate éclair while being sexually stimulated."

HEY BABIES

What do you worry about? Probably you worry about things like this:

- Where's Mommy? I can't see Mommy!
- No! Not creamed spinach again!
- Is it time for poopy?

But has Mommy ever failed to come back? Do you have any control over the creamed spinach? When is it *not* time for poopy?

Wise up, babies. Later on you'll have *real* problems.

If yoga was outlawed, then only outlaws would have flexible well-toned bodies and the radiant glow of inner peace.

Why don't you slip into something more comfortable? Like me.

Sorry that your order of ham and eggs is taking so long. The chef still can't catch the pig, and the prep cook is still shaking the chickens.

When I was a young boy, I never understood my father's love of fly fishing and his need to leave our family to embark on annual trips to Montana. Finally I understood when I was old enough to accompany him on one of his trips where he introduced me to the experience of Montana's abundant trout streams and brothels.

In a delightful new children's book, Bob the Badger leaves his meadow because "everybody fucking pisses me off" but eventually learns the lesson that he cusses too much for a character in a children's book.

Hi there, I'm the actress who does those commercials where I look like I'm having an orgasm when I discover that the new dishwasher leaves my dishes spotless. I just want you to know that in real life I'm a regular person with down-to-earth values who only has orgasms while sitting on my washing machine during the spin cycle.

I looked for happiness in fast living, but it was not there. I tried to find it in material possessions but it was not there either. I checked fast living one more time and I guess I didn't look hard enough the first time.

Feeling lonely because you don't have a "special someone" in your life? Be patient because somewhere out there is somebody made just for you, even if that "special someone" takes a long time to inflate.

Acknowledgments

Huge thanks to Kristen, Julia, Jessica, Sara, Tonya, and Sofi.

You helped me decide which jokes to keep and, more importantly, which jokes to bury deep underground so nobody will ever see them.

About the Author

Scott Erickson is an award-winning writer of humor and satire. He has found that writing satire is very challenging because civilization keeps coming up with things that are more absurd than he can make up.

He has done some interesting things in his life. He spent 5-1/2 months backpacking around the biggest lake in the world, lived for 1-1/2 years at a rural not-for-profit institute teaching sustainable living skills, and spent a summer helping friends establish an organic farm.

He enjoys roller skating and drinking beer, but not at the same time. He is possibly the nicest curmudgeon you'll ever meet.

More information can be found at
www.scott-erickson-writer.com